Hugs and Sprinkles

The Cupcake Club

Also by Sheryl Berk and Carrie Berk

Hugs and Sprinkles

The Cupcake Club

Sheryl Berk and Carrie Berk

sourcebooks
jabberwocky

Published by Sourcebooks Jabberwocky, an imprint of Sourcebooks, Inc.
P.O. Box 4410, Naperville, Illinois 60567-4410
(630) 961-3900
Fax: (630) 961-2168
www.sourcebooks.com

Library of Congress Cataloging-in-Publication data is on file with the publisher.

Source of Production: Versa Press, East Peoria, Illinois, USA
Date of Production: February 2017
Run Number: 5008745

Printed and bound in the United States of America.
VP 10 9 8 7 6 5 4 3 2 1

Shall We Dance?

"So what do you think?" Lexi Poole asked, holding up a page in a department store catalog. On it was a photo of a girl wearing a big, pale-blue, billowy ball gown—complete with a rhinestone tiara. It was supposed to be a weekly meeting of Peace, Love, and Cupcakes, but she couldn't help asking her friends and fellow club members for their opinion. The Blakely Elementary School spring dance was just four weeks away, and since her lifelong crush, Jeremy Saperstone, had already asked her to go with him, she had to start planning.

"I think this is the one. *The* dress," she said.

"I think it's a little royal for a fifth-grade dance, don't you?" Jenna Medina replied, rolling her eyes. "And poofy. Really, really poofy. Is that a train in the back?"

Delaney Noonan giggled. "You'll look like a giant cupcake."

Lexi raised an eyebrow. "And what's wrong with that?"

Sadie Harris nodded her head. "Maybe it's just a little over the top, Lex? And definitely too frilly for my taste."

Lexi groaned. "That's because you'll probably go to the dance in your basketball uniform!"

"Nuh-uh!" Sadie insisted. "I already went with my mom to the mall, and I have a really pretty turquoise romper to wear. Lucas, the captain of the boys' basketball team, asked me to go with him—and he's wearing a varsity sweater to match."

"*Mi madre* is making my dress," Jenna chimed in. "Hot-pink chiffon with pearls around the waist."

"Jack Yu said he asked you," Sadie gossiped. "And that you promised him a dozen mint–chocolate chip cupcakes."

"He brings the corsage; I'll bring the cupcakes," Jenna said. "Besides, he's really cute."

"It's so not fair that Blakely has a fifth-grade dance and my school doesn't," Delaney complained. "Weber Day has a trip to a dude ranch instead. I don't get to wear a pretty dress, and I'm gonna smell like horse for days!"

"What are you wearing to the dance?" Lexi asked Kylie Carson. Their club president had been very quiet during the whole dress discussion. Lexi noticed that Kylie wasn't smiling or teasing her like the other girls. She kept her head buried in her business binder.

"I'm, I'm…" Kylie hesitated. "I'm not going."

"What?" Lexi gasped. "Why not?"

Kylie held up a stack of papers. "We have so many orders to fill before then," she explained. "We're up to our eyeballs in cupcakes, and someone has to handle it all."

"And don't forget this order." Jenna read aloud from an email. "Principal Fontina wants twenty dozen cupcakes for the dance—'baked, decorated, and delivered promptly.' I quote!"

"You see? Someone needs to make sure the cupcakes get to the dance. You guys go without me, and I'll take care of it," Kylie added.

"What? No way!" Lexi protested. "We'll figure out how to get the cupcakes *and* ourselves to the dance."

"We'll all pitch in," Delaney said. "That's what we do. Teamwork!"

"Right!" Lexi continued. "There's no need for Kylie to miss the big fifth-grade dance. Unless…" She paused to consider. "Unless you don't *want* to go?"

Lexi had a sixth sense when it came to people—maybe because she had been shy for so many years and did a lot of watching and listening instead of talking. PLC had helped bring her out of her shell and given her confidence, but she was still really good at reading what someone *wasn't* saying. Kylie was always enthusiastic, always the first person to rally their club and convince them that anything was possible if they worked together. It wasn't like her to simply back out of a good time unless she had a good reason.

"Don't be silly," Kylie said. "Of course I want to go. It's just that I can't. I'm PLC's president, and I have to hold down the fort. So you all go and don't worry about a thing. My dad said he'll help me with all the deliveries."

She glanced at the clock on the wall of the teachers' lounge. "Where's Herbie?" Their club adviser wasn't particularly punctual—he was always busy with his robotics class—but it wasn't like him to be thirty minutes late to a meeting.

"Oh! I forgot! I ran into Herbie in the hallway. He said he would be a little late. He had a robotics emergency," Sadie recalled.

"A *little* late?" Kylie sighed. "We only have the teachers' lounge for fifteen more minutes!"

"I'll go find him," Lexi said, flipping to a page in the magazine with a gold sequined gown on it. "You focus on dresses and the dance, and I'll be right back."

Before Kylie could protest, Lexi jumped out of her seat and raced down the hall to the robotics lab. She knocked on the door, but no one answered.

"Hello?" she said, opening the door a crack. "Herbie?"

A boy with dark curly hair and glasses was seated at a laptop. Lexi had seen him in one of her art classes, but he'd never said a word to her—just grunted.

"Mr. Dubois had to go get something," he said without ever looking up from the screen.

"Well, he's late for our cupcake club meeting, and I didn't see him in the hall," Lexi said. "Do you know where he might be?"

The boy shook his head. "Nope. And I'm stuck trying to reprogram Connie with no power until he comes back."

"What's Connie?" Lexi asked.

The boy took off his glasses and rubbed his temples. "Not *what*. Who. Connie is a state-of-the-art robot."

"You name your robots?" Lexi tried not to laugh.

"Well, of course. Doesn't everyone?" the boy replied.

Just then, Herbie came charging in. "I found it! I found the piece that we needed."

He brushed past Lexi and began tinkering with a mess of wires inside a metal box.

"What is that?" Lexi asked, leaning over Herbie's shoulder.

"*That* is Connie's brain," the boy answered. "And this takes a lot of concentration, so you might want to leave…" He pointed to the door.

He went back to what he was doing and handed Herbie a complicated sketch of the robot's circuitry.

"Wow! Did you draw that?" Lexi continued. "You're a talented artist!"

"And Lexi would know," Herbie said. "She's the one who makes all of PLC's cupcakes look beautiful."

"Cupcakes have nothing to do with robots." The boy waved her off again. "You should leave. *Now.* Before you break something."

Herbie mopped his brow with the back of his sleeve. "I think we're all good for the moment—no more short circuit. So I'll leave you in charge here, Arnold, while I go join the cupcake club for our meeting."

"Whatever." Arnold sniffed.

As they walked down the hall, Herbie apologized. "Arnold can be a little intense," he said. "He's all about robots, kind of like how you guys are all about cupcakes."

Lexi nodded. "I get it. Temperamental artist. When I'm

painting or drawing, I don't like to be interrupted either. It distracts my creativity."

"Exactly. But it's no excuse for rudeness," Herbie replied. "I'm trying to work with him on his manners. He's better with robots than he is with people."

"Speaking of people…" Lexi said, stopping him before they entered the teachers' lounge. "Kylie's kind of acting weird."

"Weird? How weird?"

"Well, not herself. I can't really explain it. She's just not smiley Kylie, and I don't know why."

"We all have our bad days," Herbie assured Lexi. "Like today, when our robot started smoking and short-circuited, and Principal Fontina screamed at me for setting off the second-floor fire alarms…"

"I get it. I get it," Lexi said. "Maybe something's bugging Kylie."

"Precisely," Herbie said. "And luckily, people don't short-circuit like robots. Because that was one big mess to fix."

Lexi secretly wished she could fix Kylie as easily as Herbie and Arnold had fixed Connie. But she suspected it would be a much more delicate operation.

2

Cupcake Calculations

When Lexi and Herbie finally got to the teachers' lounge, Kylie had already been through most of the agenda: several birthday parties, one retirement dinner, a baby shower, and her dad's accounting firm's annual dinner.

"We're thinking something with numbers," Sadie said, handing Lexi the order form. "'Cause ya know accountants deal with math. Yuck."

"It isn't yuck," Jenna insisted. "Pre-algebra is my best subject."

"Well, it's my worst," Sadie said. "Sometimes my dyslexia turns the numbers around."

"It must be very difficult," Herbie said, patting her on the back.

"I'm not dyslexic, and I still get my math homework wrong," Delaney said. "Like, *all* the time."

"So we should really make this order a math lesson,"

Herbie suggested. "If we need six hundred cupcakes by next Friday, and it takes an hour to bake and decorate five dozen at a time, how much time do we need to get it done?"

Sadie scratched her head. "Well, six hundred cupcakes is fifty dozen. And fifty divided by five is ten…"

"Ten hours," Kylie said. "We need ten hours to get the order done."

"Then I'd suggest you schedule two work sessions, five hours each, toward the middle of the week," Herbie said.

"It says here your dad wants devil's food and French vanilla," Sadie added. "We're pros at those."

"We could do a little calculator made of fondant on top of each cupcake," Lexi suggested. "How cute will that be? With little white tapes coming out of them."

"I like it." Kylie nodded. "I think my dad would too. All in favor, say 'Frosting!'"

"*Frosting!*" the girls shouted in unison.

"Then this meeting of PLC is officially adjourned," Kylie said.

"Not so fast." Jenna stopped her. "We didn't talk about the fifth-grade dance order. What are we doing for that?"

"Oh, the dance," Kylie said. "I thought we were done talking about it."

"It's four weeks away, but that doesn't mean we don't need to plan," Herbie reminded her.

"You see?" Lexi whispered in his ear. "Weird!"

"Flavors," Jenna said, pulling out a sheet of paper. "Talk to me about flavors." As the club's taste tester, the ingredients and flavors were her biggest concern.

"Maybe cotton candy cupcakes for the dance?" Delaney suggested. "With little puffs of real cotton candy on top?"

"Oooh, love that!" Lexi said. "I've always wanted to work with spun sugar."

"And chocolate–peanut butter cup—always a crowd pleaser," Sadie added. "With peanut-butter filling in the middle."

"*Delicioso!*" Jenna replied. "Smooth, not chunky, of course. We need one more flavor, and we're *perfecto*."

The girls looked to Kylie, who was staring at a blank page in her binder. So Jenna elbowed her. "*Qué pasa?* Why the long face? This whole dance thing has really gotten your goat."

"I don't have a goat," Kylie replied. "But that's actually not a bad idea. Maybe a strawberry cupcake with goat cheese frosting."

"Done and done!" Jenna said. "I'll make up a list of ingredients, and we can shop next week."

As the girls packed up, Lexi continued to notice that Kylie didn't seem like herself. Anytime anyone mentioned the dance, she got quiet and sad.

"You hate my dress—just say it," Lexi said to her. "That must be it. You don't want to tell me and hurt my feelings."

"What? No. Your dress is beautiful. Big and fluffy like our cotton candy cupcakes, but beautiful."

"Then what is it?" Lexi pressed her. "You can tell me, Kylie. I'm your BFF, remember?"

Kylie took a deep breath and blurted out, "I don't have anyone to go with. No one asked me. No one likes me."

"Kylie, you know that isn't true!" Lexi told her.

"I don't mean you or the girls in our club. I mean boys."

"Herbie's a boy…" Lexi tried to argue.

"I mean a fifth-grade boy, not our club adviser. You have Jeremy, and Sadie and Jenna both have dates. I can't go to the dance alone. It would be too humiliating."

"Well, it's not too late to get a date. You have almost a month."

Kylie frowned. "Even if I had a year, I couldn't get a boy to like me."

Lexi put her arm around her friend. "Kylie, you're an amazing person. You just need a little confidence. Trust me,

I know. Remember when I would practically faint every time a teacher called on me to talk in front of the class?"

"This isn't about being shy," Kylie insisted. "It's about someone liking me for who I am: a cupcake-baking, monster-movie-loving, not-all-that-coordinated person."

"So you trip sometimes. And you can't really dance or roller-skate or ride a hoverboard. So what?"

"Lexi, I appreciate your pep talk...I think," Kylie said. "But it won't change the facts. There is not a single boy in Blakely Elementary who finds me appealing."

She gathered her backpack and left the room, slamming the door behind her.

Lexi felt just awful! Why had she brought up the dance and her dress? Why had she rubbed it in Kylie's face? There had to be some way to make her best friend feel better! Someone would surely like Kylie if they got to know her. But there was no easy recipe for cheering her up, no magical mixture that would put a smile on her face and make her feel like going to the dance.

Unless...

3

Guess Who

Kylie opened the door to her locker, and a small pink envelope tumbled out. On it was the phrase "From Your SA" with a heart drawn around it. Sadie and Jenna snuck up and peered over her shoulder. "Whatcha got there?" Jenna asked.

"What's an SA?" Kylie said, picking up the envelope.

Jenna scratched her head. "Spirit Animal? Step-Aunt? Slimy Anteater?"

Kylie wrinkled her nose. "An anteater? Really? I'm not even sure they're slimy."

"They eat bugs, don't they?" Sadie pointed out. "It doesn't get slimier than that. What's up with the initials?"

Kylie held up the envelope. "This was in my locker."

"Well, what are you waiting for? Open it!" Jenna said excitedly.

Kylie gently tore open the flap and pulled out the note card. It read:

> Dear Kylie,
>
> Roses are red,
> Cupcakes are sweet,
> Being your boyfriend would be such a treat!
>
> Love,
> Your SA

"Duh! SA! Secret Admirer," Jenna said, slapping her on the back. "Kylie, that's awesome. Someone likes you."

"What? Who?" Kylie stammered, reading the note again.

"That's why they call it a secret admirer," Jenna said. "You're not supposed to know till they reveal who they are. *Muy romántico.* So romantic."

"*Muy* confusing!" Kylie said. "What am I supposed to do with this?"

Sadie shrugged. "Wait till SA makes his next move. And watch for any suspiciously behaving boys."

Kylie spied Arnold coming down the hallway. He was

so busy reading his textbook that he bumped into several people before stopping at Kylie's locker.

"You!" he barked when he spied her. "Kylie Carson."

Kylie gulped. "Me?"

"You and your cupcakes stole Herbie away from me yesterday, and now I have a Connie catastrophe on my hands. She won't work, not even with the new part Herbie found, and the robotics competition is only three weeks away."

"Are we supposed to know what you are talking about?" Jenna asked impatiently.

"Mr. Dubois has no time to coach my robotics project because he's always busy baking!" Arnold fired back.

"Herbie doesn't bake—he advises." Kylie tried to be polite. "I'm sorry if that causes you a problem."

"Oh, it does! It causes me a huge problem," Arnold replied. "I have no robot! Who cares about stupid cupcakes anyway?"

So much for politeness; he'd just insulted PLC—and cupcakes! Kylie took a deep breath. "I care. And all the people who order thousands of our cupcakes care. Maybe your robots are all you think about, but cupcakes are very, very important."

Arnold smirked. "I mean, let's be real here, Kylie. Cupcakes aren't going to change the world, but my robot might."

"Cupcakes can change the world!" Kylie said, raising her voice a little too loudly. "They make people happy. They put a smile on everyone's face! Except maybe yours!"

Principal Fontina came out of her office to see what the commotion was about and found Arnold and Kylie nose to nose in the middle of a heated argument.

"Settle down, settle down," the principal said, stepping between them. "Unless someone wants to start the day in my office."

They both backed down, and Arnold headed off in search of Herbie—but not before he glared once again at Kylie.

"Wow, he really doesn't like you!" Sadie said.

"Or maybe he does?" Jenna pondered. "I'd call that suspicious behavior, wouldn't you?"

"Arnold? You think Arnold Schweigel is my SA?"

"Stranger things have happened," Jenna said. "Jack Yu put a spider on my head in kindergarten, and now look—he's my dance date."

"Kylie Schweigel. It has a nice ring to it, don't you think?" Sadie teased.

"No. No, I don't," Kylie answered.

"Even if it's not Arnold, someone out there is writing you poetry—with cupcakes in it," Jenna reminded her. "I say, sit back and enjoy it till Prince Charming presents himself."

Kylie considered. "But what if he doesn't? What if he stays secret and admiring forever?"

"There are worse problems to have," Jenna said. She pointed to the envelope Kylie was still clutching. "I'd say that *el amor está en el aire*—love is in the air!"

☆ ☮ ☆

At lunch that day, Kylie showed the note to Lexi. "Well, whoever it is has an artistic touch," she said. "That's really nice penmanship."

"I made a list," Kylie told her fellow PLCers at the lunch table. "It's of all the boys in fifth grade."

"Oh, I get it," Lexi said. "So we go through them, figure out who is already accounted for as a dance date, and see who that leaves as your anonymous admirer."

"Exactly!" Kylie said. She took out a yellow highlighter and began going through the names.

"What about Peter Keller?" she asked.

"He's on the boys' soccer team," Sadie asked. "Which means he's already asked out one of the girl soccer players."

"Will Parker?" Kylie continued.

"He's in my history class," Jenna said. "And I know he's been crushing on Meredith Mitchell all year. His parents and her parents go to the same country club, and he always sits in the front row at Meredith's hip-hop club showcases."

"He runs around after her like a puppy." Lexi chuckled. "Arf! I'd say he's taken."

"What about Rodney Costello? He's in my English class, and he asked once if he could share my Shakespeare book."

Lexi's eyes brightened. "I know he just asked Emily out and she said no. Could be!"

Jenna held up her hand. "But Bella said yes. I saw her hugging Rodney at recess yesterday."

Kylie sighed. This was not getting her any closer to figuring out her potential date.

"Which brings us back to Arnold." Sadie pointed to one of the few names still remaining on the list. "He's available. And his initials backward are SA. Maybe it doesn't stand for Secret Admirer. Maybe it's Schweigel, Arnold!"

"Pullease," Kylie said. "He hates my guts. And he's obnoxious."

"Oh, I second that," Lexi chimed in. "He was really rude when I went to get Herbie for the meeting."

"He's really rude, period," Kylie said. "And conceited. And stuck-up."

"Conceited and stuck-up are the same," Lexi reminded her.

"Yeah, well...he's doubly stuck-up!" Kylie insisted. "He practically bit my head off and said cupcakes were unimportant."

"I wouldn't cross him off your list," Jenna said. "Boys have a really funny way of showing they like someone. They pull your hair or tease you..."

"Or call your cupcakes stupid," Sadie added.

"I'm just sayin'... He might be covering," Jenna said. "Sneaky."

Kylie turned to Lexi. "Do you think so? Do you think it could be Arnold?"

"I don't think you should worry about who it is. Just that someone really thinks you're special, Kylie."

"This is way more romantic than Jack Yu asking me out with an Oreo cookie," Jenna said.

"Or Lucas sending me an email," Sadie said.

"Or Jeremy asking my dad if he wouldn't mind driving us to the dance—before he ever asked me!" Lexi recalled. "You're right. Kylie wins. Her guy is the most romantic by far."

Kylie smiled, and Lexi breathed a sigh of relief. At last, the old smiley Kylie was back!

"Do you think SA likes monster movies? Because that's a must…"

"Sometimes opposites attract," Jenna assured her. "Jack hates peanut butter, and I have peanut butter and banana sandwiches for lunch practically every day. So there ya go." She held one up and took a big bite out of it.

"I just wish I knew more about him," Kylie said. "Or even what he looked like."

"He's a man of mystery," Sadie said. "I think that's cool."

Kylie nodded. "Yeah, I guess you're right." She balled up the list of boys and tossed it in the garbage. "Maybe it's more fun not knowing—at least for a little while."

She scanned the cafeteria, noting a few boys casually glancing in her direction. Or were they checking out the menu over the salad bar behind her? She couldn't tell. But she preferred to think that one of them was secretly dreaming of taking her to the dance.

Lexi read her mind.

"Whoever he is, he'd be really lucky to go with you," she said. "And don't you forget it."

4

I Spy

The next morning, Kylie couldn't wait to get to her locker. But this time there was nothing inside it. Instead, a fake shrunken head with bulging eyeballs was tied to the padlock. Attached to it was a note that Kylie immediately opened:

Dear Kylie,

Monsters are creepy.
Ghosts go "Boo!"
I hope you know
how much I like you!

Love,
SA

She couldn't wait to find Lexi before their math class to fill her in.

"You won't believe what he gave me," Kylie said, shoving the shrunken head in her friend's face.

"Eww!" Lexi shrieked. "What is that thing?"

"Are you kidding? It's the most thoughtful gift anyone could give me! SA knows me. He really, really knows me."

Lexi smiled. "Okay, if you're happy, I'm happy," she said. "But I think that's really gross. Couldn't he send flowers or chocolates or something?"

"I'm going to name him Sal," Kylie said, dangling the head in the air. "Get it? *SA*, then add an *L*?"

"Wait! You're naming the creepy head? Don't you think that's going a little too far?" Lexi asked.

Kylie was practically floating on air when she walked into their math room and settled into her seat.

Her teacher, Mr. Kimmel, was busy explaining quadratic equations, but Kylie barely heard a word.

"Do you think he's a fan of Bela Lugosi? Or Lon Chaney? Or Vincent Price?" she whispered to Lexi.

Lexi shrugged. She had no idea who those people were. But she had a hunch they were all actors in Kylie's favorite old monster movies.

"I wish I could talk to him. Ask him!" Kylie said dreamily.

"Aren't the notes enough?" Lexi asked.

"Are you kidding? They're just the icing on the cake. I'm going to figure out who he is. Just you wait!"

Every day for a week, Kylie raced to her locker to find yet another note tucked inside. Each one professed how special she was—and how much her admirer liked her:

> Dear Kylie,
>
> I think you're totally cute and great
> and deserving of the perfect date.
> A monster movie and cupcakes would
> be fun!
> Hope you know I like you a ton.
>
> Love,
> SA

Sometimes he left a little present tied to her lock—a glittery skull key chain, a bouquet of lollipops, a bag of chocolate kisses.

Dear Kylie,

Hearts and treats don't begin to say
how much I think of you every day.
I know you're wondering who I might be.
For now, you'll have to wait and see.

Love,
SA

"But I can't wait to meet him!" Kylie confessed to Lexi in math.

"Well, it sounds like you have to," Lexi said, reading the last note. "Besides, isn't it more fun *not* knowing?"

"No!" Kylie shouted. "It's torture! I have to know!"

Mr. Kimmel looked up from his notebook. The class was supposed to be silently solving equations. "Kylie Carson? Did you have something you wanted to say?"

Kylie shook her head. "Nope." She looked at Lexi and winked. Sure, she wanted to say something. She wanted to tell the whole school—if not the whole world—that she had a secret admirer.

When the bell rang for the next period, Kylie grabbed Lexi by the hand.

"Okay, I have a plan," she said. "So SA leaves me notes and presents in the morning, right? Before I come into school and go to my locker?"

"Right," Lexi said. "What's your point?"

"We need to get here earlier than he does. We need to be hiding and watching to see who goes to my locker."

Lexi looked concerned. "You mean spy? Jump out and then scare the guy off?"

"No! Just quietly watch and see who he is."

"I dunno, Kylie." Lexi hesitated. "How do we even know what time he comes in?"

"Well, we get here even earlier. Six a.m. We'll ask Herbie if he could let us in. He's always here super early working on his robotics inventions before Principal Fontina gets in and starts yelling…"

"Six a.m.? I don't even get up till seven!" Lexi exclaimed.

"I *know* you're a morning person, Lex," Kylie insisted. "You're always here before me."

"But six a.m., Kylie? I'll be a walking zombie all day."

"Ooh! Do you think SA likes zombies? Vampires? Frankenstein's monster?" Lexi sighed. There was no convincing Kylie otherwise. Tomorrow they would be there, waiting and watching, when SA left his next note.

Herbie was happy to let them in early—especially when Kylie insisted it was a major cupcake emergency. "I can't find the white chocolate–raspberry cupcake recipe we need for the dance," she told him. "I think I might have left it in my locker. I need to make sure before we start hunting for a whole new one."

Herbie was a little preoccupied with getting Connie the robot up and running in time for the statewide competition. "It's fine. Just don't get me in trouble—more trouble—with Principal Fontina," he said. "If you need me, I'm in the lab."

Kylie pulled Lexi along behind her. "If we hide here, he won't see us," she said, ducking behind two recycling bins at the end of the hall.

"Herbie?" Lexi asked, stifling a yawn.

"No! SA. And we have the perfect view of my locker."

They waited patiently, but no one came. It was nearly seven thirty when the rest of teachers started to pour into the school.

"Do you think he slips the note into my locker through a crack?" Kylie said. "Or maybe he figured out my locker combination."

Lexi closed her eyes and rested her head on Kylie's shoulder. "Doubtful."

"He could have been watching over my shoulder one day, and I never even knew!" Kylie speculated. "He's really sneaky—but in a sweet way."

"I didn't know you could be sneaky and sweet at the same time," Lexi said.

"Okay, maybe sneaky is the wrong word. Clever. Smart."

"Try 'really good at keeping you guessing,' which is not easy to do—trust me!" Lexi added.

By eight fifteen, almost all the students were in school and checking their lockers or chatting before class started.

"I don't get it. Do you think he knew we were spying on him?" Kylie asked.

Lexi got up from their lookout. "I doubt he's psychic," she said. "He probably just has something else planned for today. Maybe he wants to mix things up a little."

Kylie opened her locker and checked every nook and cranny. There was no note or gift, inside or out.

"Maybe he changed his mind. Maybe he doesn't like me anymore?"

"Kylie, you can't go crazy if he doesn't write. Maybe he had a test this morning—or a ton of homework."

"Or he found another date for the dance," Kylie said.

Lexi took her by the shoulders and shook her. "Snap out of it. The president of PLC is strong, smart, and confident. She focuses on her business. She eats, sleeps, and breathes cupcakes."

"You're right," Kylie said. "I've gotten so swept up in this whole love-note business that I've been neglecting our club."

"There ya go!" Lexi said. "We should meet after school and try out some new recipes."

"Ooh! I wonder what SA's favorite flavor of cupcake is?" Kylie said. "Do you think he likes chocolate or vanilla? Or something more exotic, like pineapple upside-down cupcakes?"

Lexi sighed. "Kylie, you're doing it again."

"Fine. My house. Three thirty. Tell the girls to bring their aprons."

5

Friendly Feud

Kylie checked her locker at least a dozen times during the day, but SA never left his mark.

"It's not like him," she complained to Sadie as she set up the ingredients on the kitchen counter. "Don't you think it's strange?"

"I think this recipe is strange," Jenna said, holding up a card. "Chocolate chipotle? I'm all for *caliente* spices, but I think this could set your tongue on fire."

"I thought we would mix things up a little," Kylie said.

Lexi remembered she had suggested that was SA's motivation as well. "What does this one say? Kiwi bacon?" She made a face. "That sounds really disgusting."

"Don't knock it till we try it," Kylie insisted. "I'll go get my binder so we can take notes."

She brought her book into the kitchen, and a small pink envelope fell out of it.

"What's this?" Kylie asked, picking it up.

"Don't tell me…" Jenna said. "Romeo hid a love letter in your PLC binder?"

"You see!" Lexi said. "He didn't forget you."

"How'd he get it in there?" Sadie asked.

"I had it in my schoolbag all day. So he must be in one of my classes and snuck it in!" Kylie said.

"What does it say? What does it say?" Delaney could barely contain her excitement.

Kylie read:

> Dear Kylie,
>
> Tonight I hope you'll check your TV.
> You'll see a special message from me.
> Channel 3, 9:00 p.m.
>
> Love,
> SA

Kylie ran for the remote and switched on the TV cable guide. "What's on at 9:00 p.m. on channel three?" she exclaimed, flipping through the grid. She landed on a movie title: *The Phantom Creeps*.

"Okay, that's not creepy…" Delaney said, shuddering.

"It's a Bela Lugosi movie. He's telling me he likes Bela Lugosi films just like I do."

"Or he's telling you that he's a phantom and a creep," Jenna said. "Did you ever consider that?"

"I'm sure Kylie's right," Lexi said, elbowing her. "He means it to be sweet."

"Sweet and creepy," Jenna muttered under her breath.

"Now can we get back to baking?" Lexi pleaded. "The chipotle chocolate awaits. I could do some cute little sombreros out of fondant on top."

"I can't. I have to figure out where this love letter came from."

"It came from someone who doesn't want you to know who they are…yet," Lexi said. "Can we just leave it at that?"

She dragged Kylie back to the kitchen where they tried both recipes, mixing the batter till it was smooth. Jenna made sure the spicy hot pepper gave the chocolate cake a slight heat.

"It's really good," she said. "These would be awesome for Cinco de Mayo."

"What do you think about the kiwi bacon?" Delaney

asked, handing her a cupcake that Lexi had frosted with a white buttercream flower.

"It's tangy, and it has a bit of smoke to it," Jenna said. She handed it to Kylie. "What do you think?" She waved it under her friend's nose. "Earth to Kylie. Come in, Kylie."

"Huh? What?"

"Take a bite and tell me what you think."

Kylie wrinkled her nose. "You know, I'm just not that hungry."

"Not hungry for cupcakes?" Delaney felt Kylie's forehead. "Are you sick? Are you hallucinating? Have aliens abducted you?"

"I'm fine," Kylie insisted. "I'm just not really in the mood for cupcakes."

Lexi gulped. This was worse than she'd thought. This whole secret-admirer business was ruining their cupcake business, and it had Kylie confused and distracted.

"Kylie, that's enough," Lexi finally said. "I thought having a boy crushing on you would lift your spirits and make you feel more confident, but it's destroying everything."

"What do you mean destroying everything?" Kylie asked. "You're just jealous, Lexi. You wish Jeremy was as thoughtful and romantic as SA. You wish he understood you as well as SA understands me."

Now she had gone too far. "Kylie, SA understands you better than anyone because he—I mean, she—is your best friend." Lexi paused. "It's me. I was pretending to be your secret admirer."

"You *what*?" Kylie bellowed. Her face turned bright red. Lexi had never seen her so angry.

Jenna gulped. "Lexi, you didn't!"

"What do you mean, you were pretending?" Kylie continued.

"I made it up. I put the notes and the gifts in your locker. I snuck the letter into your binder during math. I just wanted you to be happy!"

Tears filled Kylie's eyes, and she ran upstairs to her bedroom and slammed the door shut behind her.

"I get why you did it," Delaney told Lexi. "You were trying to help. But now she feels worse than before."

"I didn't mean for this to happen," Lexi explained. "I honestly thought I would send her one note, and it would make her smile and realize that someone liked her. I didn't think she'd get so caught up in it."

"It wasn't just one note," Jenna scolded her.

"I know. I couldn't stop. Every time I tried, she'd get upset, and I'd have to do another and another and another!"

"You should go talk to her," Sadie said, steering Lexi toward the staircase. "Fix this before it ruins your friendship—and our club."

Lexi went upstairs and knocked gently on Kylie's bedroom door. "Can I come in?" she asked softly.

"Go away!" Kylie shouted back. "I never want to talk to you ever again."

Lexi braced herself and opened the door. "Kylie, I know you're mad…"

"Mad? That doesn't begin to explain how I feel! I'm angry, I'm devastated, and I'm humiliated!"

"But I didn't mean for this to happen!"

"You purposely lied to me and made me look like a fool in front of everyone."

"I just wanted to make you feel better about yourself!" Lexi pleaded with her.

"By pretending to be a boy who was interested in me? By proving to me that no one really is interested or ever will be?"

"That isn't true, and you know it," Lexi said, choking back tears.

"Well, you're not one to talk about what's true or not true. I thought you were a true friend. I guess I was wrong about that too." She pointed to the door. "Get out."

Lexi left the room, closing the door behind her. She felt just terrible and didn't blame Kylie one bit for hating her. She hated herself too for letting it get this far.

"She's still so mad?" Delaney asked when Lexi came back downstairs.

"She said I'm not her friend."

"Oh, Lexi, you know she doesn't mean that," Sadie said, putting an arm around her friend. "You and Kylie are BFFs. She'll forgive you."

Lexi shook her head. "I don't think so. I think she wants me out of PLC—and her life—for good."

6

Robot Romance

Lexi figured that Kylie would probably give her the cold shoulder, but she didn't think Kylie would take the idea so literally. When they were working on their latest order—a milk-and-cookies cupcake for a tenth birthday party—Kylie "accidentally" dumped a measuring cup of ice-cold milk down Lexi's back.

"You did that on purpose!" Lexi cried, her shirt now soaked in milk.

"I slipped," Kylie said without apologizing. "Butter-fingers."

Lexi fumed. She knew Kylie wanted to ban her from PLC, but the other girls wouldn't let her. So Lexi would just have to sit there and take whatever punishment Kylie doled out.

Sadie handed her a towel. "You know she'll get over it eventually, right?" she whispered.

"When? It's been a week already!"

Kylie continued to ignore Lexi—in class, in the lunchroom, even in their PLC meetings. When Lexi tried to suggest decorations for their orders, Kylie pretended not to hear her.

"I love the idea of doing little alphabet blocks on the baby shower cupcakes—don't ya think?" Lexi asked her.

Kylie stared right over her head. "All in favor of rubber duckies?" she asked.

The girls nodded, afraid to get between them.

Not even Herbie could convince Kylie to cool down. "Lexi made a poor choice, but her heart was in a good place."

"Yeah, like the heart that she drew around the words *Love, SA*?" she asked.

"I told you... She hates me," Lexi whispered to her club adviser. "And I don't know how to fix things."

Herbie sighed. "I think it will take time. It's an open wound right now. And wounds take time to heal."

"Well, can't you do something?" Lexi pleaded with him. "Put a Band-Aid on it?"

Herbie thought for a moment. "I'm not sure I can repair the tear between you two. But at the very least, I can get her mind off it for a few days." He went over to Kylie. "I have a small favor to ask you..."

The last place Kylie expected to find herself was in the robotics lab—with Arnold! And he didn't seem too thrilled about it either.

"It was Herbie's idea that we make Connie a cupcake baker," he explained, ushering Kylie into the computer lab. "Not mine."

"It's brilliant," Herbie assured them both. "No one has ever made a cupcake-baking robot. It will win the competition—trust me."

"A robot can't bake," Kylie said.

"Why would a robot *want* to bake?" Arnold griped.

"Because it's unique, clever, and difficult to execute," Herbie explained. "In short, a prizewinning project."

"Let me say it again," Kylie repeated. "A robot can't do what PLC does."

Arnold had heard the word *prizewinning* so now his interest was piqued. "Oh, but she can. Connie can mix, frost, pipe, even sprinkle. Anything you can do, she can do better. Once I program her to do it. But I'll have to start all over while Herbie works on her wiring."

"And where do I come in?" Kylie asked. "I don't know anything about robots or computers."

"You're going to teach Connie how to make cupcakes," Herbie said. "Or rather, you'll teach Arnold. You'll tell him each of the steps that goes into making the perfect, delectable treat. And when Connie's done, she'll serve the judges her final product and blow them away."

Arnold groaned. "I wanted a robot that folds paper airplanes...or translates German...or changes kitty litter."

"Been there, done that," Herbie said. "Cupcake baking is much more original. The judges will be very impressed with something they've never seen before."

"If you say so." Arnold relented. "I just wanna win."

Herbie handed him a baking apron. "And you will— once you teach Connie how to be a member of Peace, Love, and Cupcakes."

☆ ☮ ☆

It took Kylie three days of working after school to help Arnold put together a program that would make Connie go through all the steps needed for cupcake creating.

"No, no, no," she said, as he programmed Connie to dump two cups of flour in a bowl before mixing in the baking soda and baking powder. "First, you have to combine all the dry ingredients in a separate bowl. Then you *slowly* add a little of the mixture, then a little milk to the mixer."

"Why does it have to be so complicated?" Arnold groaned. "Just put in the ingredients, mix it up, and pop it in the oven."

"Because the batter will be lumpy. Then it won't rise properly, and some cupcakes will be flat instead of fluffy. It's a domino effect. Everything has to be done just right."

Arnold hit Delete on his laptop. "Fine, start over. Give me the steps again."

The robot would crack the eggs, sift the flour, cream the butter and sugar, pour the batter into a muffin pan, put the cupcakes in the oven, take them out, then frost each cupcake to perfection once they were cooled.

"Okay," Arnold said, once he had all the information input into the program. "Now let's give her a try."

Connie looked more like a washing machine than a baker; she had lightbulbs for eyes, mechanical claws for arms, and wheels under a short, square body that was filled with wires, buttons, and switches. She beeped and buzzed as she moved around, but Arnold spoke to her like she was human.

"There, there, Connie," he said, coaxing her. "Raise those arms a little higher so you can open the oven and get the cupcakes on the top shelf."

"Does she ever answer you?" Kylie taunted him. "Or talk back and tell you to stop pushing her buttons?"

"No, but I understand her. I hear her loud and clear."

Kylie rolled her eyes. "You don't say."

"I do say!" Arnold replied. "We understand each other perfectly. Here, you try."

He handed Kylie a remote control and motioned for her to speak into it. "Tell her to crack the eggs. She responds to voice commands."

"Crack the eggs," Kylie said, trying not to crack up herself.

"No," Arnold instructed her. "Politely."

"Connie," Kylie said. "Will you please crack the eggs gently on the side of the bowl—and be careful not to get any shells in the batter?"

"Your commands have to be short and direct," he corrected her.

"Tap egg on bowl," Kylie tried.

Connie's eyes lit up.

"Okay, that's a little spooky," Kylie said.

The robot sputtered, then spun around, reaching for an egg on the counter.

"Oh my gosh," Kylie said. "She's doing it. She's actually doing it!"

"I told you she would if you asked nicely."

They watched as the robot gingerly cracked an egg on the side of the bowl. The whites and yolk oozed out, and there wasn't a shell in sight.

"Wow. That's incredible!" Kylie exclaimed.

"That's Connie," Arnold replied. "You think she needs a chef's hat?" He took the one Kylie had brought and tried it on the robot's head. "I think it might make her feel more official."

"Feel? Robots can't feel…can they?"

"I think so," Arnold said. "Sometimes I think they're more feeling and compassionate than a lot of people. People can be mean and inconsiderate."

Kylie nodded. "*Some* people." She thought of Lexi. "But a robot can't really be your friend."

"Well, when you don't have a lot of friends like me, robots are just fine for company," Arnold said.

For the first time, Kylie actually felt a little bad for him. "You don't have friends? How come?" She took a seat next to him as he tinkered on his laptop.

"I dunno. I guess I'm just too busy for friends. For anything really."

"I get that," Kylie said. "I'm really busy with school and homework, and then there's PLC. Sometimes I feel like I have no time for anything either. Like I'm just spinning my wheels—like Connie."

"And kids in school… Well, they think I'm different," Arnold said. "I don't really fit in."

Kylie remembered when she first came to Blakely in fourth grade. She had felt the same way. It was the reason she'd started PLC—to bring together a group of people who all needed a place to fit. "Different isn't bad," she told Arnold. "It's okay to be different. It's what makes you special."

Arnold gulped. "You…you think I'm special?"

Kylie smiled. "I do."

Arnold blushed. "I think we should call it a day. I don't want to fry her circuits." He hit a button, and Connie shut down.

"Aw," Kylie said. "I was having fun."

"With robots? You?" Arnold teased her.

"Yeah, me."

When she left the robotics lab, Kylie reached for her phone, then stopped herself. She really wanted to call Lexi and tell her that Arnold wasn't as bad as he seemed. In fact, he was pretty nice. Then she remembered: she and Lexi weren't friends anymore.

Herbie spotted her in the hall. "You miss her, don't you?" he asked.

Kylie quickly shoved the phone in her pocket. "Miss who?"

"Lexi. Your best friend. You wanted to call her."

Kylie shrugged. "I forgot…for a minute."

"Maybe you should forget for more than a minute," Herbie suggested. "Forgive and forget."

Just then, Lexi walked by on her way to art class.

She looked down, careful not to make eye contact with Kylie.

"Hey," Kylie said softly.

Lexi looked up, surprised. "Hey." She smiled. Was there a thaw in Kylie's cold shoulder?

"Now, that's music to my ears!" Herbie said, beaming. "Two friends, saying *hey* in the hallway, just like old times. Kylie, is there anything else you wanted to tell Lexi?"

Kylie shrugged. "No. That's all." She marched to her English class without another word.

"Well, it's a start," Herbie said, trying to reassure Lexi. "She misses you, you know."

"I miss her too," Lexi said.

"Give it a little more time."

Lexi was happy to give it a little time—as long as it didn't take forever.

7

BFF Reboot

Together, Kylie and Arnold worked every day at lunch and recess and after school, whipping Connie into a cupcake connoisseur.

"Did you see how she piped that last one?" Arnold asked Kylie. "With that little flourish at the end?"

Kylie held up the cupcake. "It's a masterpiece. Even Lexi couldn't do better than that." She winced when she realized she'd mentioned her friend's name.

"So, what's up between you and Lexi?" Arnold asked. "I mean, you two were really tight—and now you make a face when you say her name."

"She did something really mean," Kylie replied.

"On purpose?"

"Well, yes…and no." Kylie considered what Lexi had done.

"There is no yes and no," Arnold corrected her. "It

was either on purpose, or it wasn't. Like when I program Connie: I either put in the command or I don't. Although sometimes, I kind of goof up and make a mistake…"

"Lexi goofed up and made a mistake," Kylie said, interrupting him. "A horrible mistake. And it hurt my feelings and made me look stupid."

"Well, you don't look stupid now. I think you're really smart, Kylie."

Kylie felt her cheeks turning red. "You do?"

"I mean, of course I do. You're a cupcake rock star. If I win this robotics competition, it's because of you. Connie and I would be lost without you."

Kylie wanted to hug him. That was the nicest thing any boy had ever said to her. "That's really sweet, Arnie."

Arnold's eyes grew wide. "Arnie? No one has ever called me Arnie before."

Kylie gulped. She hadn't meant to offend him! "I'm sorry! My friends shorten my name sometimes and call me Kyle or Kyles, and my dad calls me Smiley Kylie…"

"No, I like it," Arnold replied. "It's just that I've never had anyone call me a nickname—not a nice one, anyway. Sometimes the guys in the boys' locker room call me Bot Boy or Four-Eyes."

"Well, now you have a real nickname." Kylie smiled. "I'll call you Arnie from now on."

Arnold blushed. "Thanks."

She tried to change the subject. "I guess we should clean up, huh?"

"Nope," Arnold said, hitting a few buttons on his laptop. "Connie has that all under control."

Kylie watched the robot not only pick up a towel from the counter but also wipe down every inch until it sparkled.

"I taught her the command 'Clean,'" Arnold explained. "Cool, huh?"

"Very cool! We could use her help after PLC has done a big order. You should see the mess our club makes!"

"I bet," Arnold replied. "Maybe sometime I could come over and see you guys in action."

Kylie smiled. "Of course! That would be awesome!" Then she blurted out: "Are you going to the fifth-grade dance?"

Arnold bit his lip. "Um, no. You?"

"No," she replied. "No one asked me, so I guess not."

"You could take Connie," Arnold teased. "She's a really good dancer."

Kylie raised an eyebrow. "No way. She dances too?"

"Wanna see?" Arnold typed in a sequence on his computer,

53

and Connie immediately began whirling and twirling around the room, waving her arms in the air.

"That's amazing!" Kylie said, laughing. "She's really graceful."

"I taught her to do the 'Whip/Nae Nae' dance," he said. "She's got serious moves."

"What else can she do?" Kylie asked.

"What *can't* she do? She can spell, do math, speak Mandarin and French and Spanish…"

"Oh, Jenna would love her. They could *habla* all day long!"

"She can shoot a basketball into a hoop…" Arnold continued.

"And play a game of one-on-one with Sadie!" Kylie enthused. "Awesome!"

"I programmed her once to paint a still life of a bowl of apples."

"Lexi would just love that!" There—she'd said her friend's name. And it didn't make her sad or mad at all.

"Connie's pretty amazing," Arnold said, patting the robot on the head. "Good girl."

"*You're* pretty amazing," Kylie told him. "You're going to be really famous one day. I know it." She looked past his glasses into his eyes, which were a deep, dark blue.

Arnold blushed. "You think so? I mean, no one has ever called me amazing before either."

"Well, no one ever made a cupcake-baking robot before," Kylie said. "So that makes you cool in my book."

"Can I ask you something?" Arnold began. He touched her hand, and Kylie held her breath. Maybe he thought her mentioning the dance was an invitation for him to ask her? She hadn't meant it that way—or had she?

"Do you want to come with me Saturday to the robotics competition? You know, just in case Connie needs some expert advice? Or I need a vote of confidence?"

Kylie considered his request carefully and smiled. "Yes, but only if I could bring one of my friends since you're bringing your friend Connie." She knew exactly who she wanted to invite.

☆ ☮ ☆

Lexi couldn't believe her ears when Kylie called her. "Me? You're inviting me? I thought you hated me!"

"*Hate* is a strong word," Kylie said. "I was mad at you, but I was also mad at myself. I got too carried away and let that get in the way of everything."

"So what changed?" Lexi asked.

"I found a not-so-secret admirer." Kylie giggled.

"No way! Who?" Lexi gushed.

"Arnold."

Lexi's jaw dropped. "Seriously? Bot Boy?"

"He's a lot more than that," Kylie explained. "He's sweet and sensitive and really, really smart."

"And he likes you! Of course he does! Why wouldn't he? You're all those things too, Kylie."

"I didn't think I liked him. I mean, he was kind of obnoxious when we fought at my locker that time. But he grows on you."

"Like a weed?" Lexi teased.

Kylie chuckled. "I guess. We just spent the whole week working on Connie together, and I really think I like him and he likes me."

"So, what are you waiting for?" Lexi pushed. "Ask him to the dance."

"Ask *him*? I can't. I mean, I hinted, but I can't be the one to ask."

"Why not? You're a modern woman!"

"I just can't. I don't want to scare him off."

Lexi thought for a minute. "Then someone needs to give him a little push."

"Lex, please don't meddle in my love life again. We both know that doesn't end well," Kylie begged her. "I forgive you. Now promise me you won't do anything or say anything to Arnold."

"I promise," Lexi said. She had no intention of giving Arnold a push—but she knew someone else who might be willing to lend a hand.

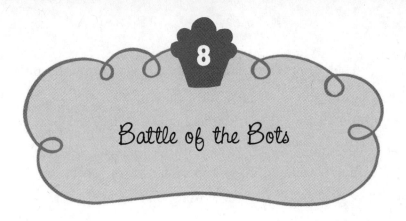

8

Battle of the Bots

The robotics competition looked like something out of a Star Wars movie. There were all kinds of beeping, blinking robots around the room—some with heads and bodies, and others that resembled vacuum cleaners.

"This is really...*different*," Kylie said, surveying the room. "I've never seen anything like it." Each team was working out the last-minute kinks on their robots. "Whoa! That one looks like R2-D2, don't ya think?"

Arnold didn't hear a word she was saying. He was too busy checking and double-checking Connie's internal memory card and the program he'd created on his laptop for her to follow.

"Arnie, you're all set," Kylie said, trying to assure him. "You've been over it and over it."

"Well, I should go over it again," he said, ignoring her. "One more time."

Herbie rolled up behind them, pushing a cart filled with measuring cups, assorted bowls, muffin tins, and piping bags. "You want to give it a once-over?" he asked Kylie. "Make sure Connie's got all her cupcaking equipment ready?" Thankfully, he was a lot calmer than Arnold.

Kylie looked over everything and nodded. "Everything's here."

"You're sure?" Arnold grabbed her by the shoulders. "You're absolutely positive *nothing* can go wrong?"

"Well, I never say *nothing*," Kylie confessed. "I mean, there was that time when Lexi accidentally forgot to pack the piping bags and we had to frost all the cupcakes at the last minute with Sadie's skateboard key…"

"What? Do you have the piping bags?" Arnold rifled through the cart.

"Yes, yes," Kylie said. "That was just a Lexi oopsie. It happens."

"Did I hear my name?" Lexi asked. She was carrying several boxes of prebaked cupcakes for Connie to decorate when the time arrived.

"I was just telling Arnold about the time you frosted eight dozen cupcakes with a skateboard key."

Lexi laughed. "Yeah, that was an oopsie. The annual

kite-makers' convention. But it's no worse than the time I had to use a ketchup bottle to pipe roses!"

"Oh yeah," Kylie recalled. "The Ladies of Litchfield luncheon. I forgot the piping-bag *tips* that time, and you improvised. That was an epic oopsie."

"What? Epic oopsies? That cannot happen today. Do you hear me?" Arnold was now hyperventilating. "Everything has to go exactly as planned and programmed."

"It will." It was Herbie's turn to try to calm him. "You've done an amazing job, and your program is flawless."

"But is it amazing and flawless enough?" Arnold asked, checking out his competition. "I mean, look at that obstacle-course navigator the Westport team came up with. It's sick!"

"Looks pretty healthy to me," Kylie said, poking Arnold playfully in the ribs. "Get it? Sick? Healthy?"

Arnold was not in the mood for jokes. Not when the Darien team had built a sumo robot that could actually wrestle. "I feel a little faint," he said. "Is the room spinning?"

Herbie helped him sit down on the floor and place his head between his knees. "Take a deep breath," he instructed Arnold. "You're going to be fine."

"Fine? I don't want to be fine. I want to win. I have to win!"

Lexi pulled Kylie aside. "Wow, your boyfriend's intense," she said.

"He's not my boyfriend," Kylie corrected her.

"*Yet*," Lexi replied.

"Arnie's just worried," Kylie said. "I get it. He has so much riding on this, and he put his whole heart into it."

"His *whole* heart?" Lexi teased. "I hope he saved some of it for you. Did you mention the dance again?"

Kylie shook her head. "No, I can't. He's a wreck. Any more pressure might drive him over the edge." She walked off to help Herbie line up all the ingredients on the demonstration table.

Lexi noticed Arnold tinkering with a walkie-talkie-like gadget. "What's that thing do?" she asked.

"This *thing* helps me communicate with Connie," he explained. "She can respond to voice commands. If anything goes wrong with her preprogramming, I can correct her and she will follow my orders."

"No kidding?" Lexi asked. "So if you said, 'Connie, paint the *Mona Lisa*,' she'd do it?"

"I'd have to program that skill set," Arnold explained.

"Right now, I could say, 'Connie, go right, go left, raise your arm' and she'd do it. Or, 'Spin three hundred and sixty degrees in a direction—'"

"Could she give someone a little push?" Lexi interrupted.

"A push? I suppose," Arnold replied. "I'd have to command her to raise her arms and move forward."

"Uh-huh," Lexi said. "That's fascinating."

He set the remote down on the table. "Don't touch it," he warned Lexi. "It's highly sensitive."

Lexi placed her hands behind her back. "Of course!"

She waited patiently for Arnold to walk away, then quickly grabbed the remote and put it in her pocket. All she had to do was get Arnold and Kylie next to each other for her plan to work. She watched as the two of them got Connie ready for her moment in the spotlight. Kylie tied an apron around the robot's waist, and Arnold placed a measuring cup in Connie's hand. They worked quickly and efficiently, but every time Kylie went right, Arnold seemed to go left. There was no getting them together long enough for Connie to give them a push.

"Students, advisers, and robots," a voice boomed over the loudspeaker. "The annual Connecticut Robotics

Competition will begin in two minutes. Please take your places."

"That's your cue to take your seat in the bleachers," Herbie said, ushering Lexi off the gymnasium floor.

"Really? So soon?" Lexi pleaded with him. "Couldn't I just stand on the sidelines and watch?"

"Not a chance. Arnold would have my head," Herbie insisted. "Only the robotics teams and advisers are allowed on the floor. No spectators."

Lexi pouted. How was she supposed to see her plan through all the way from the top of the bleachers? Like the time she piped roses with a ketchup bottle, she would simply have to improvise.

9

Clean Up Your Act

Lexi watched anxiously as several teams presented their robots. One zoomed around the floor doing its version of *Swan Lake*. Another walked a narrow tightrope on a single wheel. Finally, it was Arnold and Kylie's turn to show what Connie was capable of.

"This is Connie, and she bakes cupcakes," Arnold announced in the microphone. A hush fell over the gymnasium. He flipped a switch on Connie's control panel, and she began emptying a measuring cup filled with flour into a mixing bowl. Each time Arnold handed her another ingredient, she poured it in without spilling a drop.

He rolled her over to the next station. Connie scooped the batter into a muffin tin that he and Kylie had lined with cupcake wrappers. Each scoop had the perfect amount.

"This is going really well," Kylie whispered to Arnold. "Don't ya think?"

"Don't jinx us," Arnold whispered back. "But yeah."

Finally, it was Connie's chance to demonstrate her piping abilities. As Lexi watched, Arnold stood next to the robot, and Kylie watched over his shoulder. The piping bag was already in Connie's hand when Lexi saw her opportunity and seized it.

"Turn *right*," Lexi spoke into the remote. The robot suddenly obeyed and faced Arnold.

"Connie! What are you doing?" He looked panic-stricken. "The cupcakes are in front of you. Start piping!" He went to his laptop and punched a few buttons, but the robot refused to turn around. He searched the counter for his remote. "Where is it?" he asked Kylie. "I left it here! It's the only way I can override her."

"Now *push*!" Lexi said from her seat in the bleachers, mentally urging the robot to give Arnold a gentle nudge right into Kylie's arms. Instead, Connie's eyes flashed and her head started to shake from side to side. She looked confused.

"I said, *push*!" Lexi repeated into the remote. Connie just stood there, beeping.

"Oh, wait! Forward! Go forward!" Lexi tried. "Isn't that what Arnold said? Go forward?" This time, Connie inched ever-so-much closer to Arnold and Kylie.

"Okay, now arms up!" Lexi said excitedly. It was working! Connie raised her arm—but the piping bag was still in her hand.

"Put that down! What are you doing?" Arnold scolded the robot. He tried punching the buttons on her control panel, but it was no use.

Herbie raced to his side. "Are her circuits overloading? Does she have a short?" he asked.

"She's like a zombie," Kylie said. "Why won't she listen to what you programmed her to do?"

"I have no idea!" Arnold cried. "And the judges are watching every move!"

Lexi waited till the perfect moment—when Arnold was facing Connie and Kylie was next to him—to issue her final command. "*Push!*" she said into the remote and crossed her fingers. But instead of giving Arnold and Kylie a gentle nudge, Connie squeezed the piping bag. Pink frosting went flying right into Arnold's face.

"Stop! Stop!" Arnold cried, finally cutting off Connie's power switch. The robot's eyes went dark, and her arms fell to her sides.

"I'm finished! Ruined! The judges are going to deduct a million points from my score!"

Kylie felt awful; they had worked so hard for this day! And somehow, something had gone wrong, terribly wrong. Epically wrong. This was no oopsie—it was a train wreck! She gazed up at the bleachers and saw Lexi watching them. She noticed there was something in her hand—Arnold's remote! And when Lexi realized Kylie had seen it, she quickly tucked it in her pocket.

"Oh my gosh, she was trying to get us together," Kylie said.

"Who? What? Get who together?" Arnold said.

"Connie. I mean Lexi. That was the plan. She didn't mean to mess things up…"

Arnold scratched his head. "I have no idea what you're talking about."

"Just follow my lead, okay?" Kylie said. "Trust me, Arnie. I've got this."

She grabbed the microphone and took a deep breath. "So you all know that little messes always happen when you're baking cupcakes in the kitchen," she said, addressing the audience and judges. "Flour flies; frosting winds up on your face…"

She turned Arnold around to face the audience. "See? What do you do when you get icing up your nose?" Everyone roared with laughter.

Arnold was mortified—then caught on to where Kylie was going with this.

"You clean it up!" he said. He hit a few buttons on his laptop, and Connie sprang back to life. She picked up a towel from the counter and then wiped Arnold's face till it was spotless.

There was thunderous applause in the gym—and the lead judge came over to congratulate Arnold and hand him a prize ribbon. "A robot that bakes and cleans up the kitchen afterward—very clever," he said. "And something we've never seen before."

As he walked away, Arnold pulled Kylie into a huge bear hug. "That was amazing! You totally saved our presentation!"

"*Our* presentation?" Kylie asked.

"Well, yeah," Arnold said. "We're a team."

Lexi raced down from the bleachers the second she saw her bestie and Arnold hugging.

"It worked!" she said. "Kinda. I mean the frosting in the face wasn't great…"

"It was!" Kylie said. "The judges were totally wowed, and we never would have thought of it."

"Can I have my remote back?" Arnold asked Lexi, holding out his hand.

Lexi pulled it from her pocket. "Sorry. I just wanted you guys to get together. I wanted Kylie to have a date for the dance."

Arnold smiled. "Oh. So that was the plan. Why didn't you just say so?" He turned to face Kylie. "Would you go to the dance with me? If I promise to leave Connie at home? I guess she is kind of a third wheel…" He hit a button, and Connie spun around. "Get it? Wheel?"

Kylie laughed. "I get it, and I would love to go."

Lexi put her arm around the robot. "Nice job, girl-friend," she whispered to Connie. "We did it!"

The Icing on the Dress

Kylie stared in the mirror in Lexi's bedroom. "I dunno about this dress. I think I look weird." She was wearing a navy dress with a round collar and long sleeves.

Lexi shook her head. "It's not weird, it's just a little… plain," she said, tugging at the hem. "And long and shapeless."

"It looked really good when I ordered it online. I thought it would be dark and dramatic. But on me it looks…ugh."

"Maybe you just need a little makeup," Lexi suggested. She applied lip gloss, mascara, and pale-pink eye shadow to Kylie's face with an artistic touch.

"There!" she said. "So much better."

Kylie wrinkled her nose. "Well, my face looks better. But my dress is still awful. It just doesn't feel like me. The model was way taller—and curvier." She fussed with the too-long sleeves and baggy waistline.

There was a knock on Lexi's bedroom door, and Jenna

bounded in. "*Hola, chicas,*" she said. She was wearing the hot-pink ruffled dress her mother had made her. "How do I look?" Jenna asked. She twirled around, and the layers of chiffon flew out in every direction.

"Stunning," Lexi said. "Like a beautiful flower."

Kylie looked down at her drab dress. "Ugh," she said and sighed again.

"*Qué pasa?*" Jenna asked, noticing her. "Are you going to a dance or a funeral?"

Kylie buried her head in hands.

"We're having a bit of a fashion emergency," Lexi explained.

"You can say that again," Jenna muttered under her breath.

"I didn't have a lot of time to find a dress," Kylie said. "Not with us having to bake two hundred and forty cupcakes for the dance and get them all packed and ready to deliver."

"So you chose *that* dress?" Jenna chuckled. "Was it on sale...or free?"

Lexi elbowed her. "It's not *that* bad. Really."

Jenna shook her head. "Lexi is a really bad liar. It's that bad, *chica*. I'm telling it to you straight."

Sadie was the last to arrive and was waiting downstairs when the girls finally emerged from Lexi's room. She was wearing a turquoise romper that showed off her mile-long legs.

"Whoa, you look gorge!" Lexi gushed. "That color is beautiful on you."

Sadie blushed. "Really?"

"You all look lovely." Lexi's mom beamed. "So grown-up!" Then she noticed Kylie's long face. "What's wrong, honey?"

Kylie flopped down on the couch. "You all just go to the dance without me. I can't go looking like this."

"You cannot stand Arnold up," Lexi reminded her. "We'll figure something out."

"Is a whole new dress not an option?" Sadie asked.

"An hour before the dance?" Kylie exclaimed. "No. Not an option."

Lexi sat down next to her and picked up her sketchbook and pencil off the coffee table. "You're like a naked cupcake," she said.

"Naked? You want me to go naked to the dance?" Kylie shrieked.

"No!" Lexi insisted. "I mean you're like a naked cupcake that needs a little frosting and decoration to dress it up and make it a masterpiece."

"I could ask my mom to bring over some trim and her sewing kit," Jenna volunteered.

Lexi smiled. "Sadie, go get the scissors in my desk drawer."

"Scissors? What are you going to do with scissors?" Kylie gulped.

"We're going to give your dress an extreme makeover, PLC style!"

☆ ☮ ☆

It took Jenna's mom twenty minutes to gather up all her materials and drive over from across town. Lexi was anxiously watching the clock when she rang the doorbell.

"Thank goodness, you're here!" she said, pulling Mrs. Medina inside.

"*Mami, prepárate,*" Jenna advised her. "Prepare yourself. This dress is a mess."

Kylie stood up and spun around. Jenna's mother's jaw dropped.

"I know, I know. It's awful!" Kylie said, embarrassed. To make matters worse, Lexi had cut about six inches off the hem and chopped the sleeves off.

"*Dios mío!*" Jenna's mom said. "Where do I begin?"

"I sketched it out," Lexi said, jumping in. "It needs

some trim here, some tapering here, maybe some gold braid and lace…"

Mrs. Medina looked over Lexi's design and finally nodded. "*Sí, es posible.* But I'll need you girls to stand back." She took out a cushion filled with pins and began working fast and furiously on Kylie's dress.

"Don't move," Jenna told her friend. "You don't want to get stuck. When my mom gets in the zone, she's a little crazy with a needle."

It took another thirty minutes for Mrs. Medina to shorten the hemline and sleeves, take in the waist, and stitch delicate gold-sequin trim around the collar. She also added a touch of navy lace that flowed off the shoulders like delicate petals, as Lexi had sketched. Just then, the bell rang again.

"That's my secret weapon!" Lexi said, racing to get the door.

In walked Delaney, dragging a large suitcase. "I wasn't sure what you needed, so I brought everything," she said.

"What? What did you bring?" Kylie asked nervously.

"My entire costume trunk from all my school musicals!" she said. "Jewelry, shoes, hats, you name it…I've got it all."

"You're like a one-woman department store!" Sadie exclaimed, taking a chic black faux-fur stole from the bag.

"I remember when you wore this in *Bye Bye Birdie*. And these!" She found a pair of old-lady spectacles and placed them on the tip of her nose.

Lexi shoved her aside. "Let me see what we can use to frost—I mean, accessorize—Kylie."

She chose a delicate gold-beaded headband, rhinestone earrings, a pair of gold strappy sandals, and an elegant navy satin evening bag with a gold clasp. "This should do it."

The girls and Mrs. Medina stepped back to admire their handiwork. "*Qué bonita!*" Jenna's mother said, proud of the job they'd all done. "So beautiful!"

"Kyles, you look like a million bucks," Delaney chimed in.

"You look like one of our cupcakes." Lexi giggled. "Which is a good thing."

She walked Kylie over to the large mirror hanging in the foyer. Kylie's face lit up. "I'm not ugh anymore!"

"No," Lexi said, hugging her. "You're gorgeous."

"And we have ten minutes to get to the dance," Sadie said, noting the clock. "Before Principal Fontina kills us for being tardy with her catering order."

"Everybody hop in the car," Lexi's mom said, grabbing her keys. "Can't keep the boys waiting!"

Kylie held them back for one quick group huddle. "Thank you all," she told her clubmates. "And the moms too. What would I do without you guys?"

Jenna tugged her out the door. "Look like a naked cupcake going to a funeral," she teased. "*Vámanos!*"

"Eye" Like You

When they got to the Blakely gymnasium, there was a disco ball on the ceiling. "This is so cool," Sadie said, admiring the twinkly lights and streamers. "It's hard to believe it's the same place I shoot hoops all the time."

The theme of the dance was Lighting Up the Night, and Herbie had done a great job of "electrifying" the space. He'd even made huge light-up letters that spelled out *Blakely* and flashed in time to the music.

Each of the girls found their dates: Jeremy took Lexi's hand and dragged her out on the dance floor. Jack traded Jenna a pink rose corsage for the dozen mint–chocolate chip cupcakes, and Lucas, captain of the boys' basketball team, gave Sadie his favorite New York Knicks baseball cap and blushed when she put it on. Kylie scanned the room for Arnold but didn't see him.

"Oh, he'll be here," Herbie told her as he handed out cups of punch. "Trust me, nothing could keep him away. He just had a little mishap."

"A mishap?" Kylie imagined the entire robotics lab blowing up. "Is he okay?"

Herbie pointed to the gym doors. "Why don't you ask him yourself?"

Arnold walked in wearing a black suit and bow tie—and an eye patch.

"Arnie, what happened to you?" Kylie gasped, running to his side.

"Well, I guess you could say I survived a cupcake calamity," he said. "But it's okay. I'm alive to tell the tale."

"Cupcake calamity? Why were you making cupcakes?"

"For you!" He smiled and handed her a small white box. Inside was a chocolate cupcake, decorated with a piped red rose on top.

"It's like a cupcake corsage!" Kylie gushed.

"Connie and I made it, but then I got a little too close to the mixer, and flour flew in my eye. It's really red and swollen and irritated, and my mom had to take me to the eye doctor…"

Kylie chuckled. "You need some lessons," she said,

taking his arm. "Never crank the mixer to full speed until the wet and dry ingredients are blended."

"Now you tell me?"

They found Lexi and Jeremy chatting in a corner. "I keep telling her she's a really good dancer, but she won't dance with me," Jeremy said.

"Lexi just doesn't like to have everyone watching her, right?" Kylie said, linking arms with her bestie.

"Exactly!" she replied. "Kylie knows me better than anyone."

Jenna and Jack found the group as well. "Jack, share your custom cupcakes." Jenna elbowed him.

"Nuh-uh!" he insisted. "They're all mine. You guys have to get your own."

Jenna rolled her eyes. "You're gonna eat a whole dozen?"

"Nope." Jack grinned. "I was gonna give half to you."

"Oh!" Jenna giggled. "Well, that's okay then."

They spotted Sadie and Lucas slow dancing. "I don't believe it!" Lexi said. "He's taller than her. I didn't think *anyone* was taller than Sadie!"

"Should we give it a spin?" Arnold asked Kylie. "With no wheels, I promise."

Kylie gulped. "I'm not the most coordinated person,"

she admitted. "I once did a hip-hop move and kicked my sneaker off in Meredith's face."

"Then I'm lucky it's a slow dance," Arnold said. "And you're not in high-tops." He led her to the center of the gym floor.

"Oh, this is *so* adorable!" Lexi cooed. "And romantic." She pulled Jeremy to his feet. "Let's go."

"I thought you hated to have everyone watch you?" he replied, confused.

"I do. But I gotta hear what they're saying to each other!"

Jenna chuckled. "Report back," she told her friend. "I can't leave Jack with the cupcakes, or there won't be any left for me."

Lexi and Jeremy sidled up next to Kylie and Arnold. "Can you hear what they're saying?" Lexi asked her date.

"The music is kinda loud," Jeremy answered. "Do you read lips?"

"I wish!" Lexi replied. It was very frustrating, but she could see that Kylie was smiling and laughing. She looked so happy.

When the music finally stopped, Lexi pulled Kylie aside. "So? How's it going?" she asked, pumping her friend for details. "Is it a match made in heaven?"

"More like a match made in the robotics lab, but it's good," Kylie said. "Arnie said he really likes me."

"OMG!" Lexi squealed. "That's amazing!"

"I told him he could come to our next PLC meeting and bake with us."

Lexi's face fell. "You did *what*? Boyfriends don't come to PLC meetings. I've never taken Jeremy to a PLC meeting. It's club members only."

"I know," Kylie said. "But Arnie is really interested in learning to bake. He might even join now that he doesn't have so much work to do for a robotics competition."

"Join? Join our club?" Lexi couldn't believe her ears.

"I know it's really soon, but he's great and I like him." She hugged Lexi tight. "I owe it all to you. You made me realize I could have a boyfriend, Lex."

Before Lexi could say another word, Principal Fontina found them. "Fabulous job on the cupcakes as always," she told Lexi and Kylie. "I've had two of the cotton candy ones already!"

"Oh, you have to try one of the strawberry–goat cheese," Kylie insisted. "They're our new flavor!" She led her principal back to the cupcake table. Jeremy found Lexi still standing on the dance floor by herself.

"What's wrong?" he asked her. She looked like she was in shock. "Didn't Principal Fontina like the cupcakes?"

Lexi nodded. "She liked them. It's Kylie."

"Kylie didn't like them?" Jeremy asked.

"No, she likes Arnold."

"I thought that's what you wanted."

"I did," Lexi insisted. "I wanted Kylie to be happy, but not if it means destroying Peace, Love, and Cupcakes…forever!"

Boys Can Bake

Three days later, the entire fifth grade was still buzzing about how much fun the dance had been. Kylie couldn't stop talking about it—and all things Arnold.

"Did I tell you Arnie is into bugs?" she asked Lexi over lunch in the cafeteria. "The creepier and crawlier, the better."

"Bugs? Can we not talk about bugs while I'm eating?" Jenna grumped. "It's ruining the enjoyment of my mac and cheese."

"Can we not talk about *Arnold* while I'm eating?" Lexi muttered. "It's ruining *everything*."

She was sick of how Kylie's new BF was all she ever wanted to discuss. There were dozens of cupcake orders to be planned, baked, and delivered, but all Kylie had on the brain was Arnie. It was just like when she had obsessed over her secret admirer—but worse, because now he was real!

"So I was thinking of inviting him over Friday night to watch *The Fly*," Kylie continued. "It's one of my fave monster movies and very buggy."

The conversation was bugging Lexi. "Kylie, we have that delivery Sunday for the ninety-six-year-old's birthday party. We were going to bake all day Saturday," she reminded Kylie.

"Oh, that's perfect! Arnie can help us make the order, then watch *The Fly*!"

Lexi bristled. She was hoping Kylie would forget the whole idea of Arnold joining PLC. None of the other girls even seemed to mind! She waited till Kylie went to get seconds on her chicken nuggets to try to convince them this was a *very* bad idea.

"Jenna, you don't want an outsider baking with us—getting in your ingredients and stuff, right?" Lexi asked her.

Jenna shrugged. "Lex, you didn't want Delaney to join us either, and now look how important she is to PLC. I'm cool with giving Arnold a chance."

Lexi looked to Sadie. "But too many cooks spoil the cupcakes, right?"

Sadie thought for a moment. "I dunno. I mean, Arnold is really smart. How bad a baker could he be?"

They found out at noon on Saturday, when Arnold arrived at Kylie's house for his very first PLC cupcaking session.

"Okay, Mrs. Lewis requested lemon–poppy seed cupcakes with vanilla–cream cheese frosting." Kylie read the order carefully. "Arnold, you're with Sadie on egg cracking."

Sadie handed him a bowl and a dozen eggs. "Careful to crack the egg exactly in the middle with one firm tap." She demonstrated. "If the crack is clean, you won't get shell bits in the batter."

Arnold tried the first egg, and it shattered into the bowl. "Um, I think I got a few splinters in there," he said, trying to pick them out. The egg whites were way too slippery, and they kept escaping him.

"Here, you use half of the shell to scoop 'em out." Sadie showed him. "It's like a magnet. It gets them right up." Instead, Arnold dropped several whole shells into the bowl while trying to weed out the tiny pieces. He took a wooden spoon and tried to mash the shells in so no one would notice.

"Maybe you should help me on the batter," Delaney suggested. She handed him a measuring cup and the bag of flour. "It needs to be exactly one and a half cups," she said.

"No more, no less." Arnold nodded, but when he picked up the bag of flour and started to pour it into the cup, he accidentally spilled the entire pound all over the counter.

"This is a lot harder than it looks," he said, trying to mop up the mess. The more he wiped, the more the flour wafted in the air. "Connie made it look so easy."

"I'd rather Connie be here than *him*," Lexi whispered to Jenna. "He's a disaster."

Jenna took him under her wing and tried to teach him about tasting. "So when we're making lemon cupcakes, we have to be very precise about how much zest and juice goes into the batter. Otherwise, you get a really sour cupcake." She handed him a grater and a lemon. "You zest."

Arnold looked at the strange flat tool with holes in it. "I don't know how," he said. "What do I do with this?"

Lexi grabbed it out of his hand. "You scrape the out-side of the lemon carefully." Arnold spent the next half hour scraping the lemon till it filled a measuring cup with pieces of lemon rind. He dumped the entire cup into the batter.

"No! The recipe calls for two teaspoons finely shred-ded!" Delaney exclaimed.

"These are chunks," Jenna said, looking into the mixing

bowl. "*Gigante* chunks. And this is way more than two teaspoons. We'll have to toss this batter out and start again."

Lexi couldn't stand it one more minute. "Okay, enough. Arnold can't join PLC. He's ruining everything!"

"Wait! I can fix it!" he said, flipping the switch on the mixer. "If we just mix it all up, it'll be fine." He turned the speed to high, and the batter splattered everywhere.

"Stop! Stop!" Lexi said, trying to push him out of the way. The girls all stepped back because this was about to get messy.

"Oh, you're right!" Arnold said. "I forgot the poppy seeds!" He dumped a cup of seeds into the spinning mixer—and they immediately flew out as well. Lexi was now covered in lemony poppy seed goo.

"You are awful! Just awful!" Lexi cried. "You can't bake!"

"Never said I could." Arnold started laughing. "Robots are more my thing."

"And bugs!" Kylie joined in, cracking up. "Don't forget bugs."

"It isn't funny," Lexi said, trying to wipe the sticky batter out of her hair.

"Oh, it is!" Kylie insisted. "Nice job, guys." Everyone was high-fiving.

Lexi was confused. "I don't understand. You did this on purpose?"

Kylie put her arm around her. "We thought maybe we should give you a little lesson in what it feels like when someone butts into your batter."

"Oh," Lexi said. "Like how I meddled in your love life."

Kylie nodded. "Exactly. It was my idea, but Arnie and the girls agreed to help."

"You should have seen your face, *chica*, when he poured in the poppy seeds." Jenna laughed.

"Wait, so this was all a plan? You don't want to join our cupcake club?" Lexi asked Arnold.

"Huh? No way! I mean, I know now that cupcakes aren't stupid, but I'm not a baker. I'm a robot maker."

"And we like it that way." Kylie gave his hand a squeeze.

Lexi looked down at her batter-stained apron, jeans, and sneakers. "Could you have found a way to make your point without covering me in cupcake batter?"

Kylie handed her a towel. "Sorry we made a mess of your clothes."

"Sorry I made a huge mess of our friendship," Lexi said. "No more meddling. I won't even ask for any more details of your love life."

Arnold blushed. "Well, that's a relief!" He turned to Kylie. "I'll go home and leave you guys to your baking."

"Don't be late for the movie," Kylie reminded him.

"I won't! I'll bring popcorn. I googled the movie, and it looks really creepy. I'm psyched!"

Lexi waited till he had shut the door behind him to make one last comment to Kylie. "I know you don't want me meddling any more in your relationship…" she began.

"Lex, haven't you learned your lesson?"

"I have! But OMG, he likes monster movies? Kylie, he's a keeper!"

Kylie smiled. "Ya think?"

"Ahem," Jenna interrupted them. "We have a ninety-six-year-old not getting any younger who needs four dozen cupcakes in the morning. Can we please get back to baking?"

Lexi took off her dirty apron and tied a clean one around her waist. "Baking before boys!" she vowed. "Cupcakes before crushes!" And this time, she really, truly meant it.

Cotton Candy Cupcakes

Cupcakes

Makes 12 cupcakes

- ¾ cup (1½ sticks) salted butter
- 1⅔ cups all purpose flour
- 1 cup sugar
- 1¼ teaspoons baking powder
- ¼ teaspoon baking soda
- ½ cup milk
- 3 egg whites
- 1½ teaspoons cotton candy extract or flavor (I like LorAnn Oils.)
- Pink food coloring
- Light-blue food coloring

Directions

1. Have a grown-up help you preheat the oven to 350°F. Line a muffin tin with cupcake liners.

2. With a grown-up's help, heat the butter until melted in a small saucepan over medium heat, and allow it to cool.

3. In a large mixing bowl, whisk together flour, sugar, baking powder, and baking soda. Transfer these ingredients to the large bowl of an electric mixer.

4. Add milk, egg whites, and cotton candy extract, and mix all together on medium speed until smooth.

5. Add butter, and mix again until combined.

6. Pour the batter into two bowls, and use the food coloring to dye one pink and one blue. Use just a few drops, and mix and check the color before adding more. A little goes a long way, and you don't want the color to be too intense.

7. Spoon pink batter into each cupcake liner, about one-fourth full, and then add blue batter on top. Use a toothpick to swirl the two colors together. The batter should fill the liner about halfway to the top.

8. Bake for 18–20 minutes, or until a toothpick inserted in the middle of a cupcake comes out clean.

9. Have an adult remove the pan from the oven, and allow the cupcakes to cool completely, about 15

minutes, before frosting. Because the cupcake flavor is so sweet, I like a simple vanilla buttercream frosting on top.

Vanilla Buttercream Frosting

3 cups confectioners' sugar

1 cup (2 sticks) butter, room temperature

1 to 2 tablespoons whipping cream

1 teaspoon vanilla extract

Directions

1. In the bowl of an electric mixer, cream the sugar and butter together on medium speed until light and fluffy.

2. Add cream and vanilla, and continue to beat. The frosting should be smooth and spreadable. If it's too thick, add a spoonful or two more cream, checking consistency after each addition. If the frosting becomes too watery, add a little more confectioners' sugar.

Cotton Candy Toppers

1 bag cotton candy (I like Charms Fluffy Stuff.)

4 plastic straws

Directions

1. Cut each straw into three equal pieces.
2. Pull a "puff" of cotton candy from the bag, and insert the straw piece into it.
3. Poke the straw through the center of your cupcake frosting so it stands straight up. Now your cupcakes are carnival worthy!

Strawberry Cupcakes with
Goat Cheese Frosting

Strawberry Cupcakes

Makes 12 cupcakes

⅔ cup fresh or frozen strawberries, thawed

1½ cups all-purpose flour, sifted

1 teaspoon baking powder

¼ teaspoon salt

¼ cup milk

1 teaspoon vanilla extract

1 cup sugar

½ cup (1 stick) unsalted butter, room temperature

1 large egg

2 egg whites

Directions

1. Have a grown-up help you preheat the oven to 350°F. Line a muffin tin with cupcake liners.

2. With the grown-up's help, puree the berries in a small food processor.

3. In a medium bowl, whisk together flour, baking powder, and salt.

4. In another bowl, mix together strawberry puree, milk, and vanilla.

5. Cream together sugar and butter in the bowl of an electric mixer. Beat on medium-high speed until light and fluffy.

6. Reduce the mixer speed to low, and slowly add egg and egg whites until just blended.

7. Now add half the flour mixture, then half the milk mixture, then the rest of the flour, followed by the rest of the milk. Mix until batter is smooth.

8. Fill cupcake liners two-thirds full with batter. Bake for 18–20 minutes, or until a toothpick inserted in the middle of a cupcake comes out clean.

9. Have an adult remove the pan from the oven, and allow the cupcakes to cool completely, about 15 minutes, before frosting.

Goat Cheese Frosting

I like how this frosting has tanginess to it—a perfect balance for the sweet cupcakes!

8 ounces goat cheese

8 ounces cream cheese

½ cup butter (1 stick)

6 cups confectioners' sugar

1 teaspoon salt

2 tablespoons cream or milk

Directions

1. Allow goat cheese, cream cheese, and butter to sit out until they are slightly soft and at room temperature.

2. In a large bowl, combine the confectioners' sugar and salt.

3. In the bowl of an electric mixer, mix together the goat cheese, cream cheese, and butter until smooth.

4. Add the sugar and salt mixture one cup at a time.

5. The frosting should be smooth and spreadable. If it is too thick, add a tablespoon or two of cream or milk, mixing and checking consistency after each addition. If the frosting becomes too watery, add a little more confectioners' sugar.

Chocolate Cupcakes with Peanut Butter Frosting

You can bake a peanut butter cup right into the middle of the chocolate batter, or save to decorate the top of the frosting.

Chocolate Cupcakes

Makes 12 cupcakes

- 1⅓ cups all-purpose flour
- ¾ cup unsweetened cocoa powder
- 2 teaspoons baking powder
- ¼ teaspoon baking soda
- Pinch of salt
- 1½ cups white sugar
- 3 tablespoons butter, softened
- 2 eggs
- ¾ teaspoon vanilla extract
- 1 cup milk

Directions

1. Have a grown-up help you preheat oven to 350°F. Line a muffin pan with cupcake liners.

2. In a large bowl, sift together the flour, cocoa, baking powder, baking soda, and salt.

3. In the bowl of an electric mixer set at medium speed, cream together the sugar and butter until light and fluffy.

4. Add the eggs one at a time, then stir in the vanilla.

5. Add the flour mixture and the milk; alternating between them as you beat well.

6. Fill the cupcake liners two-thirds full. Bake for 18–20 minutes, or until a toothpick inserted in the middle of a cupcake comes out clean.

7. Have an adult remove the pan from the oven, and allow the cupcakes to cool completely, about 15 minutes, before frosting.

Peanut Butter Frosting

1½ cups creamy peanut butter

½ cup (1 stick) butter, room temperature

2 cups powdered sugar

1½ teaspoons vanilla

½ cup evaporated milk

Mini peanut butter cups

Directions

1. In the bowl of an electric mixer set at medium speed, beat together peanut butter and butter until smooth.

2. Add powdered sugar and vanilla, and beat until combined.

3. Add milk, beating on medium-high speed until light and fluffy. If frosting is too thick, you can add a few drops more milk—just mix and check consistency after each addition.

4. Top each cupcake with a mini peanut butter cup.

Carrie's Cupcake Crafts:
Cupcake Liner Corsages

You will need:

    8 solid-colored cupcake liners

    1 small safety pin

    1 green pipe cleaner

    Scissors

Directions

1. On a flat surface like a countertop, flatten each of the cupcake liners and then stack one on top of the other with the inside facing up.

2. Ask a grown-up to help you use the pin to poke a hole through the entire stack.

3. Take your pipe cleaner and begin threading (from outside of liner in) through the center hole.

4. Bend the end of your pipe cleaner into a little knot to secure the liners into place, then slide all the liners so they're up tight against the knot.

5. Working from the inside out, scrunch each cupcake liner around the pipe cleaner knot. The liners closer to the middle will fold in tighter, and the outside ones will be more open—just like the petals of a real flower.

6. Gently pinch and shape your corsage until you're happy with how it looks.

7. Trim the pipe cleaner with scissors so the tail is about six inches long. Wrap it around the non-pin side of the safety pin a few times and tuck it under tightly. Now pin the corsage on your favorite person!

Acknowledgments

Many thanks to all our family and friends who make "Cupcake" possible:

The Kahns, Berks, and Saperstones, as always, for their love and support. Daddy and Maddie: love you to the moon and back!

Our supersweet agents, Katherine Latshaw and Frank Weimann from Folio Lit; and our great team at Sourcebooks Jabberwocky: Steve Geck, Kate Prosswimmer, Alex Yeadon, and Elizabeth Boyer.

All of our Cupcake Club fans who come to every signing, preorder our books, and race to bookstores the day the next book is out—and share their enthusiasm for the series with us! Hugs and sprinkles!

About the Authors

Sheryl Berk is the *New York Times* bestselling coauthor of *Soul Surfer*. An entertainment editor and journalist, she has written dozens of books with celebrities, including Britney Spears, Jenna Ushkowitz, and Zendaya. Her daughter, Carrie Berk, is a renowned cupcake connoisseur and blogger (facebook.com/PLCCupcakeClub; carriescupcakecritique .shutterfly.com; Instagram @plccupcakeclub) with more than 100,000 followers at the tender young age of twelve! Carrie cooked up the idea for the Cupcake Club series while in second grade. To date, she and Sheryl have written fifteen books together (with many more in the works!). *Peace, Love, and Cupcakes* had its world premiere as a delicious new musical at New York City's Vital Theatre in 2014. The Berk ladies are also hard at work on a new series, Fashion Academy, as well as its musical version, *Fashion Academy: The Musical*, which premiered in New York City in October 2015.

Peace Love and CUPCAKES

Meet Kylie Carson.

She's a fourth grader with a big problem. How will she make friends at her new school? Should she tell her classmates she loves monster movies? Forget it. Play the part of a turnip in the school play? Disaster! Then Kylie comes up with a delicious idea: What if she starts a cupcake club?

Soon Kylie's club is spinning out tasty treats with the help of her fellow bakers and new friends. But when Meredith tries to sabotage the girls' big cupcake party, will it be the end of the cupcake club?

Book
1

Recipe For Trouble

$\mathcal{M}$eet Lexi Poole.

To Lexi, a new school year means back to baking with her BFFs in the cupcake club. But the club president, Kylie, is mixing things up by inviting new members. And Lexi is in for a not-so-sweet surprise when she is cast in the school's production of *Romeo and Juliet*. If only she could be as confident onstage as she is in the kitchen. The icing on the cake: her secret crush is playing Romeo. Sounds like a recipe for trouble!

Can the girls' friendship stand the heat, or will the cupcake club go up in smoke?

Book

2

Winner Bakes ALL

$\mathcal{M}$eet Sadie.

When she's not mixing it up on the basketball court, she's mixing the perfect batter with her friends in the cupcake club. Sadie's definitely no stranger to competition, but the oven mitts are off when the club is chosen to appear on *Battle of the Bakers*, the ultimate cupcake competition on TV. If the girls want a taste of sweet victory, they'll have to beat the very best bakers. But the real battle happens off camera when the club's baking business starts losing money. Long recipe short, no money for icing and sprinkles means no cupcake club.

With the clock ticking and the cameras rolling, will the club and their cupcakes rise to the occasion?

Book
3

Icing on the Cake

Meet Jenna.

She's the cupcake club's official taste tester, but the past few weeks have not been so sweet. Her mom just got engaged to Leo—who Jenna is sure is not "The One"—and Peace, Love, and Cupcakes has to bake the wedding cake. Jenna is ready to throw in the towel, especially when she hears the wedding will be in Las Vegas on Easter weekend, one of the most important holidays for the club's business!

Can Jenna and her friends handle their busy orders—and the Elvis impersonators—or will they have a cupcake meltdown?

Book 4

Baby Cakes

$\mathcal{M}$eet Delaney.

New cupcake club member Delaney is shocked to find out her mom is expecting twins! When her parents first tell her, the practical joker thinks they must be pulling her leg. For ten years she's had her parents—and her room—all to herself. She LIKED being an only child. But now she's going to be a big sis.

The girls of Peace, Love, and Cupcakes get together to bake cupcakes and discover Delaney is worried about what kind of a big sister she will be. She's never even babysat before! But her cupcake club friends rally to her side for a crash course in Big Sister 101.

Book
5

Royal Icing

$\mathcal{M}$eet Kylie.

As the founder and president of Peace, Love, and Cupcakes, Kylie's kept the club going through all kinds of sticky situations. But when PLC's adviser surprises the group with an impromptu trip to London, the rest of the group jumps on board—without even asking Kylie. All of sudden, Kylie's noticing the club doesn't need their president nearly as much as they used to. To top it off, the girls get an order for two thousand cupcakes from Lady Wakefield of Wilshire herself—to be presented in the shape of the London Bridge! Talk about a royal challenge...

Can Kylie figure out her place in the club in time to prevent their London Bridge—and PLC—from falling down?

Book
6

Sugar and Spice

Meet Lexi.

The girls of Peace, Love, and Cupcakes might be sugar and spice and everything nice, but the same can't be said for Meredith, whose favorite hobby is picking on Lexi. So when the PLC gets a cupcake order from the New England Shooting Starz—the beauty pageant Meredith is competing in—the girls have a genius idea: enter Lexi into the competition so she can show Meredith once and for all that she's no better than anyone else. Problem is, PLC has to make Lexi a pageant queen—and 1,000 cupcakes—all in a matter of weeks!

Have the girls of Peace, Love, and Cupcakes bitten off more than they can chew?

Book
7

Sweet Victory

Meet Sadie.

MVP Sadie knows what it takes to win—both on the court and in the kitchen. But when Coach Walsh gets sick and has to temporarily leave school, Sadie's suddenly at a loss. What will she do without Coach's spot-on advice and uplifting encouragement? Luckily, Sadie's got Peace, Love, and Cupcakes on her side. Her friends know that the power of friendship—and cupcakes—might be just what Sadie needs! Together, they rally to whip up the largest batch of sweet treats they've ever made, all to help support Coach Walsh. When the going gets tough, a little PLC goes a long way. But this record-breaking order might just be too much for the club…

Can the girls pull it together in time to score a win for Sadie—and Coach Walsh?

Book
8

Bakers on Board

$\mathcal{M}$eet Jenna.

It's "anchors aweigh!" for the Cupcake Club!

Jenna's stepdad, Leo, is taking his family on a Caribbean cruise. Unfortunately, Jenna's younger siblings get the chicken pox, leaving Leo with four extra tickets. Enter Peace, Love, and Cupcakes! Leo says Jenna's four besties can come—in exchange for baking twelve thousand cupcakes for his company's pirate-themed event. Shiver me timbers, that's a lot of icing! Now pros the cupcake-baking game, PLC takes on the challenge.

But when a freak rainstorm flares up on the night of the big event, will it be rough seas for the girls?

Book
9

Vote for Cupcakes!

$\mathcal{M}$eet Delaney.

Cupcakes for the win!

When Delaney discovers there's been a cut to the art budget, she decides it's time to make a change! The race for class president is quickly approaching, and Delaney's going to run. Her besties in Peace, Love, and Cupcakes are ready to help in any way they can. But when Delaney's demands start infringing on PLC's ability to get out their orders—and the girls' friendships—things start to get out of hand. The girls aren't sure Delaney really knows what it takes to become president...or whether she's running for the right reasons.

As the election approaches, will it be Delaney for president? Or will her campaign (and PLC) crash and burn?

Book
10